The Never

from the mist

written by
Kiki Thorpe

Illustrated by
Jana Christy

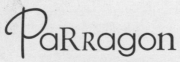

Bath · New York · Cologne · Melbourne · Delhi
Hong Kong · Shenzhen · Singapore · Amsterdam

This edition published by Parragon Books Ltd in 2015

Parragon Books Ltd
Chartist House
15–17 Trim Street
Bath BA1 1HA, UK
www.parragon.com

ISBN 978-1-4723-3131-1

Printed in UK

Never Land

Far away from the world we know, on the distant seas of dreams, lies an island called Never Land. It is a place full of magic, where mermaids sing, fairies play and children never grow up. Adventures happen every day, and anything is possible.

There are two ways to reach Never Land. One is to find the island yourself. The other is for it to find you. Finding Never Land on your own takes a lot of luck and a pinch of fairy dust. Even then, you will only find the island if it wants to be found.

Every once in a while, Never Land drifts close to our world … so close a fairy's laugh slips through. And every once in an even longer while, Never Land opens its doors to a special few. Believing in magic and fairies from the bottom of your heart can make the extraordinary happen. If you suddenly hear tiny bells or feel a sea breeze where there is no sea, pay careful attention. Never Land may be nearby. You could find yourself there in the blink of an eye.

Never Land

Pirate Cove

Torth Mountain

Pixie Hollow

SKULL Rock

Mermaid Lagoon

One day, four special girls came to Never Land in just this way. This is their story.

chapter 1

Kate McCrady opened one eye, then the other. Early-morning sunlight streamed across her face.

Kate blinked, still half asleep. Was she in her own bedroom? Was she sleeping under the weeping willow tree in Never Land? For a moment, she didn't know. She pushed a tangle of red hair out of the way and saw a large doll's house in the corner.

Oh, that's right, Kate thought. She was sleeping over at her best friend

Mia Vasquez's house. Lainey Winters was there, too, bundled in a sleeping bag a few metres away.

Kate tried to send them a silent message: *Wake up! Wake up, so we can go back!*

Only a few days before, Kate, Mia, Lainey and Mia's little sister, Gabby, had found a secret portal to Pixie Hollow, the realm of the fairies on the island of Never Land. Or rather, the portal had found them – even though the path to Never Land wasn't always in the same place, it always seemed to be where the girls could find it.

Kate loved their visits to Never Land. There she had no homework, no chores – nothing to do but explore. Adventure waited round every tree, hill and bend along Havendish Stream. Kate couldn't wait to go back.

But her silent message didn't work. Lainey let out a gentle snore. Mia turned over, burrowing deeper under her covers.

Maybe a nudge would wake them. Kate stretched so her foot grazed the bottom of Lainey's sleeping bag. She scooted closer, then stretched again. This time, she bumped Lainey's leg.

Lainey sat up, blinking sleepily.

"I was just stretching," said Kate, trying to look innocent. "I didn't wake you, did I?"

"No … yes." Lainey fumbled around by her pillow. When she found her glasses, she put them on a little crookedly. "Is Mia awake?"

"I am now!" cried Mia, pulling the pillow over her head. Kate could only see a bit of her long dark curly hair poking out. "What time is it? It feels too early to be awake."

"It *is* early." Kate jumped up, leaped over Lainey and bounced on Mia's bed. "Early enough to get back to Never Land."

Mia glanced at the clock. It said 6:30. "My parents won't be awake until at least seven."

"Exactly," said Kate. "And that could mean hours and hours in Never Land." The girls had discovered that time worked differently on their trips to Pixie Hollow. Hours could pass there, while at home hardly a minute would go by. "Let's go now!"

Mia bolted upright as a thought came to her. "I hope Gabby kept our promise. I hope she didn't try to go to Never Land while we were sleeping."

On their last visit, the portal had closed and Gabby had been stuck alone in Never Land. After that, the girls had made a promise to always go to Never Land together. But Mia was worried that Gabby wouldn't be able to resist going on her own, especially since the portal was now in her room.

The three girls dressed quickly. Kate pulled her thick red hair away from her face with a hair clip without bothering to comb it. Then she, Mia and Lainey tiptoed across the hall to Gabby's room.

Inside the door, Kate stopped short. "Do you guys see what I see?" she whispered.

Lainey and Mia nodded. A dense mist hung over half the room.

Meanwhile, Gabby slept peacefully on her back, unaware of anything unusual. Her arms were spread wide, as if she were waiting for a hug.

"She looks so sweet," Mia said softly. "Maybe we shouldn't wake her."

Suddenly, Gabby sat up. "What's going on?" she said, looking around. "Why is my room so foggy?"

"I don't know. Something strange is happening," said Mia. "Look at the wardrobe door."

A heavy mist hovered around the doorframe. More fog seemed to seep from beneath the door – the door that led to Never Land.

Kate rushed over. "I'll check it out."

"Wait, Kate. We all go together, or we don't go at all," Mia reminded her.

Kate stopped with her hand on the doorknob. "Hurry up and get dressed, Gabby."

Gabby hopped out of bed. She slipped a pink tutu and a pair of costume fairy wings over her pyjamas. "Ready!" she announced.

Kate pulled open the door. Gabby, Mia and Lainey crowded behind her.

Inside the wardrobe, fog swirled from floor to ceiling. It covered Gabby's toys and clothes. Holding hands, the girls stepped through the mist.

Kate heard a tinkling sound, like bells ringing. She took another step. Faint voices floated towards them.

"I hear the fairies!" Lainey said.

The voices grew louder as the girls crept forward. The walls around them curved, becoming the inside of a hollowed-out tree trunk.

Finally, they stepped out from the tree. They were standing on a grassy bank in Pixie Hollow. At least, Kate *thought* it was Pixie Hollow. It was hard to tell. Fog covered everything.

"I can barely see!" exclaimed Lainey. She wiped her glasses.

Kate shuffled forward a little, squinting. "There has never been fog in Pixie Hollow before. It's always sunny when we visit."

She didn't see Havendish Stream until

she almost walked into it. Now she could see the fairies whose voices they'd heard. They were water fairies paddling birch-bark canoes. The fairies called out to one another so their boats wouldn't bump.

"Watch out!"

"Where did this fog come from?"

"Go to the right, Silvermist!"

Spring, a messenger, flew over the water, shouting to the fairies. "Everyone to the courtyard! Queen Clarion has called a special meeting!"

"Oh!" She stopped inches in front of Kate. "I didn't know you girls were here. You'd better come, too!"

At the courtyard, Kate stared up at the Home Tree. The giant maple, filled with fairy bedrooms and workshops, usually sparkled with fairy glow. But today its branches were hidden by the mist.

Around the girls, fairies crowded into the pebbled courtyard. They landed on the tree branches, where they sat lined up like birds on a telephone wire. They chattered nervously, filling the air with a low hum.

"What's going on?" Kate asked a baking fairy, Dulcie, who was hovering nearby.

"Queen Clarion is worried about this fog. We all are. It is awfully strange weather for Never Land."

"What's causing it?" Kate asked.

Dulcie shrugged. "All I know is it's making the fairies hungry. At breakfast today, everyone ate like it was the Harvest Feast."

"Breakfast?" Kate's stomach rumbled. They hadn't had a chance to eat.

Dulcie winked knowingly. "I'll get you girls some treats right away!" Nothing made Dulcie happier than filling empty stomachs.

Moments later, serving-talent fairies delivered basket after basket filled with blueberry puffs. Each puff was the size of a marble, so the girls ate a lot!

Rain, a weather-talent fairy, flew by carrying a medicine dropper. She pressed the dropper's bulb to draw in some mist. Then she peered at the droplets inside.

"Sure, it's a mist easter with foggish low bursts," she announced. Then she frowned. "But squalls are down."

"Is that good or bad?" Kate asked. But she was talking to herself. Rain had already flown away.

chapter 2

Mist in the morning, fairies take warning.

Silvermist stood in the courtyard, waiting with the other fairies for Queen Clarion to speak. But her thoughts strayed.

Mist in the morning, fairies take warning. Why couldn't she get that old fairy saying out of her head?

Silvermist tucked her long hair behind her ears. All morning, she'd felt uneasy. She'd been boating on Havendish Stream when the fog came.

Silvermist had never seen such a heavy mist before. It had taken all her water knowledge to get her boat to shore without running into anything.

As a water-talent fairy, Silvermist liked water in any form – from dewdrop to rushing waterfall. Usually, just being near it soothed her. But this clammy mist made Silvermist shiver from wing to wing.

Why is it bothering me? she wondered. After all, mist was water, too.

As she thought about it, Silvermist noticed the four Clumsies kneel down behind her. *Girls. Not Clumsies,* she reminded herself. *They don't like to be called that.* She nodded hello to Kate, Mia, Lainey and Gabby.

"Hi, Silvermist," the tall one, Kate, said. "What do you think about this fog?

You're a water fairy, so you must know what's going on."

Silvermist shook her head. "I'm afraid I don't."

"Well, that's helpful," said Vidia, a fast-flying fairy, as she swept past. "A water talent who doesn't have a clue about the water right in front of her nose."

Silvermist didn't reply. Vidia always had something nasty to say. Still, the remark bothered her. Why *didn't* she know more?

Mist in the morning, fairies take warning.

"Fairies, sparrow men and guests!" said Queen Clarion, interrupting Silvermist's thoughts. "Gather close, so we can see each other more clearly."

Everyone edged forward.

"We don't know how long the fog will last," the queen said. "But it's too dangerous to fly in weather like this. There could be accidents. So for now, all fairies are grounded."

A murmur rippled through the crowd.

"What?" Vidia's voice rose above the others. "You can't mean fast-flying fairies, too? Why should we be punished?"

"No one is being punished, Vidia," the queen replied. "It's for your own safety."

"Couldn't there be exceptions?" Vidia asked, her voice sugary.

Out of the corner of her eye, Silvermist noticed Kate eagerly move closer, to see if she was 'grounded', too.

Queen Clarion thought for a moment. "You're right, Vidia. There should be a few exceptions."

Vidia gazed around at the other fairies, a superior smile on her face.

"We'll need some fairies to stay on lookout, to make sure everyone is safe," Queen Clarion continued. "The scouts – and only the scouts – may fly."

Hearing this, the fairies grumbled, especially Vidia, who scurried away using her wings to help her walk faster.

After the meeting, fairies milled around in the courtyard. They seemed nervous about going anywhere on foot.

Fawn, an animal-talent fairy, came towards Silvermist. "Have you seen Beck, or any of the other animal talents?" she asked. "We need to bring in the dairy mice but it could take ages walking. We'll have to work together to herd them."

"Can I help?" asked a voice behind Silvermist.

"Oh, Lainey, that would be wonderful," Fawn said. "You can cover much more ground than we can. And you can practise your mouse calls."

Lainey beamed, happy to be of use. She turned to Kate. "Do you want to come?"

Kate shrugged. "I don't speak Mouse. I'll find something else to do."

"Come with us!" Hem, a sewing-talent fairy, called from down by Kate's feet.

"Yes!" echoed Mia, taking Gabby's hand. "We're going to make some new doll's clothes. Hem is going to help us."

Kate shook her head. "I'm not really in the mood for sewing…." she began, when a loud rumble rolled through the sky.

All the fairies stopped what they were doing and looked up. But there was nothing to see but fog.

"What was that?" Silvermist asked.

The rumble grew louder.

Myka, one of the scout-talent fairies, took off into the soupy air. Right away, Silvermist lost sight of her.

"The fog is moving," said Myka. Her voice came down faintly through the mist. Thunder sounded again, drowning out the rest of her words. But they didn't need to hear her. The fairies could see for themselves that the fog was stirring, gathering into great big swirls.

A gust of wind kicked up. Trees swayed. The fairies clung to each other. "Is it a storm?" Dulcie cried. Storms were rare in Never Land.

Suddenly, a shrill whinny split the air.

"That sounded like it came from the meadow!" cried Fawn.

Everyone ran towards the meadow.
The fairies on the ground scrambled over
tree roots and darted round clumps of
flowers. Several fairies caught rides with
the girls, who could run much faster
with their long legs. Silvermist joined a
group of fairies riding on Kate's shoulder.

The scouts flew and arrived at the meadow first. The girls got there just afterwards. They all stood at the edge of the woods. No one wanted to go closer.

A huge cloud was rolling across the grass. It churned like rushing flood waters. The thunder was deafening. The earth trembled.

Then, as quickly as it had come up, the noise died down. The cloud blew away. In its place stood a herd of silver-white beasts with wispy manes and tails that trailed into mist. One of them shook its head. Another flicked its tail. Droplets of rain flew off them.

"Horses!" Kate murmured, her eyes widening.

"Not just horses," whispered Silvermist. "Mist horses."

chapter 3

Kate stood at the edge of the meadow, gazing at the horses. Her friends, the fairies and everything else fell away as she stared.

The horses were huge, and yet they looked as light as air. The ends of their long manes and tails seemed to disappear into the mist. Their eyes were a ghostly grey. To Kate, they looked as if they'd come straight out of the sky, as if the wind and rain had brought them to life. Even in a magical place like Never Land, the horses seemed otherworldly.

"'*Mist in the morning, fairies take warning*'," whispered a voice at Kate's ear. It was the water fairy, Silvermist.

"There's some sort of legend about the mist horses," Silvermist went on, almost as if she were talking to herself. "I think they bring trouble."

Several fairies nearby turned to look at her. "Trouble?" repeated a sparrow man, sounding worried. Others frowned.

What kind of trouble could these creatures bring? Kate wondered. They looked so beautiful and peaceful.

"You know, I'm probably confusing mist horses with sea horses," Silvermist said quickly. "I'm sure it's nothing."

The animal-talent fairy Fawn spoke up. "I'll talk to the horses. Find out where they're from and why they're here."

Fawn fluttered closer to one of the animals. She stopped so she could look it in the eye and swung her long ponytail like a mane. Then she let out a *hmph*, followed by a snort and a whinny.

Kate thought she sounded just like a horse.

But the mist creature ignored her. Fawn tried again. This time, the horse turned its back. Fawn tried another horse, but it also turned away.

Fawn sighed loudly. "They're not telling me any–"

Suddenly, one horse flicked its tail, striking Fawn.

"Oh!" Fawn spun through the air like an out-of-control spinning top.

Silvermist and Tinker Bell raced to her. They each caught hold of one of Fawn's hands. They whirled along with her until, bit by bit, they slowed. At last, they were able to land on a rock.

"Fawn, are you okay?" Tinker Bell asked.

Fawn nodded, dazed. "I – I think so."

"It's time to leave the meadow," Queen Clarion said. "It's too dangerous here."

Kate's heart sank. Leave? Now, when the horses had only just arrived? But most of the fairies seemed perfectly happy to go.

On the way back, Dulcie was already talking about the light-as-mist meringues she wanted to bake. Other fairies planned a game of hide-and-seek. "It will be extra fun in the fog!" said a sparrow man. Fawn, still too dizzy to walk, was riding on Lainey's shoulder.

Kate fell into step beside Mia. "I don't see why we have to go," she complained.

"It's probably better. They do seem kind of dangerous," Mia said with a glance at Gabby.

Dangerous? Kate thought. 'Exciting' was a better word. Of course, if you were a five-year-old – or a five-inch fairy – it was a different story. Then it made sense to stay clear of the horses. But everyone always said Kate was tall for her age. She wouldn't be in any danger.

"So now you can help us with the doll's clothes," Mia went on cheerfully. "We can start by sorting the petals and silk threads."

Mia kept talking, but Kate stopped paying attention. She really didn't want to go back to the Home Tree and sew doll's clothes. Or even play fairy hide-and-seek. The fairies, able to squeeze into knotholes or inside flower petals, always won.

Kate wanted to run and jump! She always chose football over quiet games during break-time at school. After sitting at a desk for hours, she needed to move. That was how she felt now, too.

Those horses! Kate could tell they also loved to run and jump. They were so … alive!

Kate stopped. "I'm going back for another look," she told Mia.

"What?" Mia said, startled.

"I'll just be a minute," Kate promised. "I'll meet you at the Home Tree."

Before Mia could say anything else, Kate turned and ran back to the meadow. She stood at the edge of the trees, afraid to go any closer.

The horses were still there, almost hidden in the mist. One bright, silvery mare stood at the edge of the herd. As Kate watched, the mare suddenly kicked up her hooves. She moved away from the other horses, galloping round the meadow's edge.

As the horse neared Kate, she slowed to a trot.

She sees me! Kate realized.

The mare stopped a few metres away. For an instant, Kate held her gaze. *What would it feel like to touch a mist horse?* she wondered.

Kate edged closer. Then closer still. Slowly, hardly daring to breathe, she reached out her hand. She half expected it to go through the horse, as if she were made of air.

But the mare was solid. Kate stroked her neck lightly, feeling the velvet fur and the muscle underneath.

She feels like a real horse! Kate thought. Or at least what she imagined a real horse would feel like. Kate had never touched a horse before. The closest she'd come was riding the carousel in the park near her home. But she very much wanted to ride this horse.

Kate glanced around to make sure no one was watching. If she tried to ride and then fell off, she'd be so embarrassed! Then, feeling brave and silly at the same time, she took hold of the horse's mane as gently as she could. The horse flicked her ears but didn't move.

But the mare was much taller than Kate had realized. She had no idea how to climb on!

Looking around, Kate spotted a thick tree branch a few metres above her. Maybe if she could climb the tree, she could lower herself on to the horse's back.

"Don't move," Kate whispered. She scrambled up the tree trunk, glad for the time she'd spent climbing trees in Never Land, on lookout with the scouts. Kate inched along the branch until she was more or less above the horse. The mare, nibbling at the meadow grass, didn't seem to notice.

Using all the strength in her arms, Kate lowered herself from the tree branch. Now she was dangling in the air above the horse.

"Steady now," she murmured. But just then, the horse took a step forward.

"No!" Kate gasped. Afraid it was about to run away, she let go quickly, landing squarely on the mare's back.

The horse took off. On the verge of falling, Kate reached out and grabbed a handful of the horse's long mane. She bounced all over its back. Her teeth rattled together. She expected to hit the ground at any moment. But she didn't.

At last, Kate pulled herself more or less upright. She tightened her grip on

the horse and squeezed with her knees to try to balance. The horse sped up. Kate let out a panicked squeal, but she stayed on.

"Hey!" she cried. "I'm riding!"

The faster the horse ran, the smoother her stride became. She left the meadow and headed over a hill that led to more forest.

It seemed to Kate as if they were swimming through the air. She felt a thrill travel from the tips of her toes to the top of her head. Were the horse's hooves even touching the ground? Kate couldn't tell.

"How do I steer?" she wondered aloud. Kate leaned slightly to one side, as she would to turn her bike. She tugged gently on the horse's mane. The horse began to turn.

"Yes!" Kate pumped a fist in victory.

Then she grabbed quickly for the horse's mane again. She needed to hold on with two hands to keep from falling off.

At last, the horse slowed to a trot and then to a walk. They were nearing the meadow again. "Thank you for the ride. You can go back to your herd now," Kate said.

But as they came through the trees, Kate saw that the meadow was empty. The horses were gone! In the distance, she heard whinnies and the sounds of branches snapping.

At that moment, the scout Myka swooped down from a treetop. "What are you doing here?" she asked Kate. "And on a horse?"

Kate grinned. "I was just going for a ride," she said casually. "Did you see the herd from up there?" She pointed to the tree where Myka usually stood lookout.

37

Myka shook her head. "It's hard to see anything in this fog," she admitted. "I did catch a glimpse of something moving. It could have been the horses. If it *was* them, they're heading towards Vine Grove, north of here."

"Vine Grove," Kate repeated. Perhaps she could go there, too.

Myka frowned as if she knew what Kate was thinking. "It's outside Pixie Hollow."

"I'll take this horse to her herd. Then I'll come back to the Home Tree." Kate figured that she could get to Vine Grove in no time on the horse. Then she could run back on foot before anyone missed her. "I'll be fast," she told Myka.

"I don't think that's a good idea," Myka said. "Wait here and –"

But Kate was already galloping away.

chapter 4

Silvermist hovered in front of a high shelf in the Home Tree library. She was trying to find a book about the mist horse legend.

She looked over the leaf-books on the Myths and Legends shelf. "Maybe it should be called *Mists* and Legends." Silvermist laughed at her own joke, then glanced around, afraid she might be bothering another fairy. But she was alone.

"So where might this old story be?" Silvermist said. She pulled a book from the shelf. It was titled *Hailstones in the Hollow and Other Odd Weather Fables.*

She flipped through the pages. When she saw the words 'mist horse', she stopped and skimmed the page.

"Oh, no!" Silvermist dropped the book with a thud. No wonder that warning had been echoing in her head all morning. According to the legend, the fairies were in danger!

It's just a legend, Silvermist reminded herself. Picking up the book with shaking hands, she placed it back on the shelf. *It's a story, that's all.* But Silvermist had learned that superstitious old fables sometimes had a grain of truth. If even a little bit of the legend was true, she had to warn the queen.

After leaving the library, Silvermist hurried to the Home Tree and rushed up to the queen's chambers. She knocked, but there was no answer. She tried again. Nothing.

Growing impatient, Silvermist flung open the door.

"Oh, cockleshells," she groaned. No one was there.

But through the open sea-glass window, she heard fairies talking. "I saw Kate at the meadow." Silvermist recognized Myka's voice. "She was riding a horse."

Silvermist darted back the way she'd come and went outside. Myka stood on a low branch, talking to Queen Clarion. Mia, Lainey and Gabby were there, too.

"That can't be right," Mia was saying. "Kate's never ridden a horse in her life."

"Queen Clarion –" Silvermist began. But the queen held up a hand.

"Just a moment, Silvermist," she said. "Myka was telling us something important. Are you sure it was Kate, Myka?"

"Of course I am!" Myka said. "I spoke to her. And she *was* riding one of the mist horses. She was leaving Pixie Hollow."

"No!" Silvermist gasped. This time, everyone turned to look at her.

"I went to the library," she explained. "I found an old legend about the mist horses...."

Silvermist paused and glanced at the girls. After all, the legend might not be true and she didn't want to frighten them.

"Go on," the queen said.

"Well, I read that the horses enchant their riders, so they keep riding and riding," Silvermist said.

"You mean, they can't get off?" Mia asked.

Silvermist nodded. "The rider believes the horse is loyal and obedient. But it's a trick. It's the rider who obeys the horse, as if under a spell."

"What does that mean?" Gabby squeaked in alarm.

Mia exchanged a horrified look with Lainey. "It means Kate might be in trouble."

"We have to find her!" Lainey said.

"But what about the fog?" asked Myka. "Even the scouts can't see in it."

"We'll need someone who can find their way through it," Queen Clarion said. "Silvermist, you have my permission to fly to find Kate."

"Me? Oh!" Silvermist hadn't expected to lead the mission. She started to explain that she didn't understand the fog any better than anyone else, but stopped herself. After all, Kate needed their help.

"We should leave now," she said to the girls. "The longer we wait, the harder it could be to find her. Who knows how far Kate can get on a horse. Myka, are you coming?"

Myka shook her head. "Some of the animal-talent fairies are missing. We think they got lost trying to find the dairy mice. The scouts are out looking for them."

Silvermist squared her shoulders. So she would have to lead them on her own.

"When I last saw Kate, she was heading towards Vine Grove," Myka said.

Silvermist turned to leave, but the queen stopped her, adding, "And for Never's sake, everyone, be careful."

chapter 5

"Come on, girl!" Kate urged the horse. Shapes loomed up from the mist, becoming trees and rocks that passed in a blur. Riding in the fog reminded Kate of cycling at night. She couldn't see things until they were almost on top of them. Still, the horse seemed to know where she was going. They managed not to hit anything.

As they rounded a small pond, the horse slowed. Kate reached down and patted the horse's neck. She felt like she'd been riding her whole life. And what a way to explore Never Land!

Kate looked around, trying to get her bearings. Were they close to Vine Grove? The island, cloaked in fog, seemed as mysterious as the mist horse. Kate had the feeling that anything could happen. That she could see anything. Go anywhere.

Why shouldn't I go anywhere? Kate thought. *I can explore a bit first and then bring the mare back to her herd. One little detour won't make a difference.*

Besides, Kate reasoned, there was really no need to go straight back. The horse – *her* horse – seemed to be enjoying the ride as much as she was. The longer Kate rode, the more certain of it she felt.

The horse was a wild, free creature. She made Kate feel wild and free, too.

"Let's go to the beach!" Kate cried. She turned the horse round sharply. The mare's hooves kicked up puffs of mist, like little clouds.

"Cloud," Kate said. "That's what I'll call you." The name seemed as light and free as the horse itself.

They cantered over a hill and through a grassy field. A sand dune appeared in the fog. Cloud sped up one side of the dune. Kate leaned low over the horse's neck as they raced down the other side, on to the beach.

The mist was heavier here. It rolled up to the beach with every wave.

They rode along the sand. When they came to the water's edge, Cloud whinnied loudly and charged into the surf. Waves splashed Kate's legs. She laughed out loud.

But Cloud didn't stop. Just when Kate thought she'd go under with the next wave, Cloud whirled round, taking Kate back up the beach.

Still laughing, Kate slid off Cloud's back. She removed her shoes, emptying water from them. Her jeans were soaked, but she was too excited to feel cold.

"Is anyone there?" a fairy voice called. It sounded like Myka.

Kate groaned inwardly. Now she'd have to explain what she was doing here, when she was supposed to be looking for the herd in Vine Grove.

As she opened her mouth to call back, another voice rang out. It sounded very close by, just on the other side of Cloud.

"Okay, you found me," a voice drawled with fake sweetness. "Congratulations, Myka. You caught me flying. But why go through all the trouble of tracking me down? I'm not bothering anyone here. Can't a fast-flying fairy have a little fun?"

Vidia! Kate realized. Myka hadn't been talking to Kate. She was talking to Vidia. Cloud, who blended into the mist, must be shielding Kate from their view.

"No one's trying to get in your way, Vidia," Myka said. "I was scouting for lost fairies."

"Well, I'm not lost. I know exactly where I am."

Kate stood still. She hoped Vidia and Myka wouldn't notice her. This time, Myka would insist she go back. Then Cloud raised her head and snorted.

"Are you coming down with the fairy flu, Vidia?" Myka asked. "It wouldn't be a surprise in this damp weather.

You should go home and have a nice hot cup of dandelion tea."

"I didn't sneeze," Vidia snapped. "*You* did. Don't try to trick me."

"Trick you?" Myka repeated, confused. "I'm not trying to do anything but keep you safe."

"Tell you what," Vidia said, her voice sugary again, "if you can catch me, I'll go back with you."

Kate heard the fast fluttering of wings, then Myka sighing.

Silence fell. Had Myka flown off, too? Kate waited a few moments longer, then decided she and Cloud were alone.

I'll leave now, too, Kate thought. She could take a shortcut, going round the pond the other way to get to Vine Grove. Then she'd go back to the Home Tree.

"Okay," Kate whispered into Cloud's ear. "Let's get you to the herd."

There was no tree nearby. But this time, as Kate took hold of Cloud's mane, she managed to pull herself up with only a bit of struggle. Kicking her legs, she belly-flopped on to Cloud's back, then wriggled around so she was upright.

"Is anyone else here?" Myka called. "Water fairies? Sparrow men?" She paused. "Kate?"

But Kate didn't hear her. She was on her way to Vine Grove.

*

On horseback, Kate neared a thick group of trees. Long green vines twisted round trunks and looped from branches.

"That must be Vine Grove!" Kate said.

Kate rode into the trees, following the sounds. As they went deeper into the grove, the trees grew closer together. Creeping plants covered the ground and the path became hard to follow.

Kate ducked her head as vines brushed her face. Between the fog and the leaves, she could barely see.

Ahead, vines tangled together like a thick green wall. Cloud strained through.

"Oh!" Kate struggled – pushing, pulling and batting at leaves and stems. But the vines caught her up like a net, holding her tight.

Cloud kept moving but Kate, trapped in the vines, swung into the air.

"Cloud!" she called. The horse stopped a little further ahead. She looked back at Kate and whinnied, as if to say, *What on Earth are you doing?*

Suspended in mid-air, Kate struggled
and flailed. But she couldn't free herself
from the vines. She needed Cloud to
pull her out.

She called again. "Cloud! Here, girl!"
This time, Cloud stepped closer.

Slowly, Kate worked one arm free.
She stretched but couldn't reach Cloud.
"Just a little bit closer," she coaxed. The
horse toed the ground but didn't move.

All Kate could do was throw her legs forward and back and begin to swing. With every swing, she got a little closer to the horse. At last she'd worked herself far enough forward that the fingertips of her free hand grazed Cloud's mane. One more swing and Kate flung her arm round Cloud's neck.

"Go!" she shouted.

Cloud took off, pulling Kate along with her.

The vines round Kate snapped free of the trees. The force swung her out of the vine trap and over Cloud's head, as if she were jumping from a swing when it had reached its peak. She landed hard on the ground.

Kate stood up shakily. Her hair fell into her eyes and, as she reached up to swipe it away, she realized she'd lost her hair clip. She spent a few moments searching for it, but it was nowhere to be seen in the dense undergrowth.

Kate turned in a circle, trying to get her bearings. Ahead, the trees thinned out a little. She could see the shapes of large animals moving among them. The herd!

"Go on, girl," she said to Cloud. "Your friends are right over there!"

But Cloud didn't move.

Why won't she go to them? Kate thought. Something was wrong.

Kate made her way towards the herd. As she drew closer, she could see the animals more clearly. They weren't horses after all. They were deer. She'd been following the wrong herd!

Where were the mist horses?

Kate looked to where the trees thinned out even more. *If I were a horse, I'd rather be out in the open than in a dense forest,* she thought.

"Let's keep going," Kate told Cloud. They'd find the herd. It wouldn't be fair to Cloud to give up.

And besides, Kate was having too much fun.

chapter 6

Back in Pixie Hollow, Silvermist and
the girls set off towards Vine Grove.
Silvermist flew in front. The girls walked
in single file behind her, following a
narrow path. The path was faint and
overgrown, more of a deer trail than
anything. But it was the quickest way to
Vine Grove that Silvermist knew.

Vine Grove was to the north of Pixie
Hollow. The trail went through the woods
and round a small pond. When Silvermist
came to the edge of the pond, she stopped.

There in the mud were two crescent-shaped marks. *Hoofprints!* Silvermist suddenly realized.

"What is it?" asked Mia, coming up behind her.

"There," Silvermist said, pointing. "They're from a horse's hooves, I'm sure of it."

"If the herd came this way, there'd be more tracks. So it must be from the horse Kate is riding!" Lainey said. "Let's follow them."

"The thing is, they're headed south, towards the sea," Silvermist said. "*Away* from Vine Grove."

Mia frowned. "Myka said Kate was heading *towards* Vine Grove. We should go there."

"But this is a clue!" Lainey countered. "Don't you think we should follow it?"

Both girls looked at Silvermist. She
realized they were waiting for her to
decide what to do.

Silvermist looked down at the tracks,
thinking. The hoofprints did seem like
a good sign. On the other hand, Kate
had told Myka that she was going to
Vine Grove. Which way was right?

Silvermist took a deep breath and closed her eyes. *Trust your instincts,* she advised herself. *If I were on a mist horse, where would I go?* Behind her eyelids, Silvermist saw waves crashing. She felt the tug of the sea.

Silvermist opened her eyes. "We should go to the beach," she said.

With Silvermist once again in the lead, the group set off. Before long, the woods gave way to marsh. They climbed over a dune, slipping and sliding down the soft sand on the other side. Fog still hid everything around them. But they could hear waves breaking and seagulls squawking and Silvermist knew they'd reached the beach.

"Stay close," she instructed. "We don't want to get separated in the fog."

"Kate?" Mia shouted. "Are you here?"

"Kate! Kate!" Lainey and Gabby joined in. They walked up and down the water's edge, calling and searching. But there was no sign of Kate.

"She's not here," Gabby said finally.

"Maybe we should have gone to Vine Grove after all," Lainey said, glancing at Silvermist.

Silvermist nodded, feeling a knot in her stomach. She'd been so sure that this way was right. But maybe it was only her feeling for water that had drawn her towards the sea. Maybe her instincts had let her down.

And now they had lost so much time!

"We'd better hurry," she said, "or we may never catch up with Kate."

The girls and Silvermist retraced their steps away from the beach. This time, Silvermist didn't stop to check for prints. She didn't want to waste another second.

Soon enough, they came to a thick wooded area. Long vines hung from the trees, twisting round trunks and plants.

"This must be Vine Grove!" Mia said, racing towards the trees. "Kate! Where are you?" she cried.

But once again, no one answered her.

The girls walked among the vines, looking all around. Silvermist flew close to the ground. She scoured the undergrowth for some sign that Kate had been there. But she saw nothing.

"I don't understand," Mia said. "If Kate's not here, where is she?"

Silvermist swallowed hard. "There's something I haven't told you. About the legend –"

She was interrupted by a shout.

"Over here!" Lainey cried. "I found something."

They followed Lainey's voice through a tangle of vines. Lainey stood on the other side. She pointed to the ground. "These vines were trampled."

"Something big must have done this," Mia said, examining the vines. "Maybe a horse. What do you think, Silvermist?"

Silvermist nodded. "It's possible."

A short distance away, they found another tangle of broken vines. Between the leaves, something gleamed.

"Look!" Gabby cried, bending over to pick it up. "A hair clip."

"It's *Kate's* hair clip," Mia said. "So she *was* here!"

Silvermist blushed, her glow turning orange with embarrassment. She was sure she'd flown right past this spot before.

How could she have missed something as obvious as a Clumsy's hair clip? She was starting to wonder if she should be leading the girls at all.

"Silvermist," Gabby said, "what should we do now?"

Silvermist hesitated. She couldn't trust her instincts. They had led her astray once already. She needed a real clue.

A movement among the trees made Silvermist's heart skip a beat. She turned towards it, hoping to see Kate. But it was only a deer. The deer gazed silently at them for a moment. Then it turned and bounded away, shaking droplets from the wet leaves around it.

"I wish I could speak Deer," Lainey said. "I could have asked if it had seen Kate."

"Hmm," said Silvermist, not really listening. The deer had given her an idea.

She began to fly slowly over the ground, looking closely at the leaves and blades of grass.

"What are you doing?" Mia asked.

"The leaves and grass are covered with droplets of water from the mist," Silvermist explained. "So if something as big as a horse passed through here, it would shake the water off ... like this!" Silvermist pointed to a path through the damp grass.

The girls squinted. "I don't really see anything," Lainey said.

But Silvermist could see it clearly. Each blade of grass was wet on one side and dry on the other. "A large creature has come this way."

"Are you sure it was Kate and the horse?" Mia asked. "And not a deer or something else?"

"I'm not sure it was Kate," Silvermist admitted. "But it was bigger than a deer. And right now, I'm afraid that it's our only clue. We have to keep going."

Before it's too late, she added to herself.

chapter 7

Cloud galloped down a hill covered with sweet-smelling primroses. Kate could just see the yellow blossoms peeking out from the drifting mist.

Kate giggled with delight and flung one arm into the air, as if she were riding a roller coaster. This time she wasn't afraid of falling off. "Yeehaw!" she yelled.

The ground levelled and they trotted past a noisy waterfall. The rushing water gurgled and hissed, dropping from a rocky ledge into a deep blue pool.

A butterfly fluttered in front of them. Its bright blue colour was startling in the sea of white mist. Kate sneezed and the butterfly spiralled away in the whoosh of air.

Never Land was even more amazing than Kate had imagined – animals, flowers, fog and all. She spurred Cloud on, eager to see more.

But wait, she reminded herself. *We have to search for Cloud's herd.*

And then what?

Kate had never cared much about having a pet, unlike Mia, who loved her cat, Bingo, and Lainey, who loved all animals. But now that she and Cloud were together, Kate wanted a horse. She wanted *this* horse. If she and Cloud could stay together, Kate would have days like this all the time.

Oh, if only there was some way I could keep her! Kate thought.

"Caught you, Clumsy," a voice purred in her ear.

Kate jumped. She twisted round and saw Vidia flying next to her.

"Look who's taking in the sights of Never Land," Vidia said. "Seems we're both far from home. Lost, are you?"

"Of course not," Kate snapped. Truthfully, she wasn't sure how far away from Pixie Hollow she was. But she felt certain that when it was time to return, she could find her way. "I'm taking this horse to its herd."

"I don't care much what you do," Vidia said. "But I'm heading back to Pixie Hollow. The fog seems to be getting worse in this direction."

Kate frowned. She didn't want any advice – especially not from Vidia.

"I'm not afraid of a little fog," she said. "Why should I be, when I have Cloud?"

"You really think you've trained a wild horse?" Vidia snickered.

Kate grinned. "Watch this! Go, Cloud!"

With that, Cloud took off, leaving Vidia far behind.

This time, they rode until Kate's arms and legs ached. Her belly grumbled with hunger. She hadn't had anything to eat except Dulcie's blueberry puffs, hours earlier. She thought Cloud must be worn out, too. But strangely, the horse never seemed to get tired.

When Kate spied an apple tree rising out of the mist, she stopped and hopped off the horse. She twisted two apples from the tree and held one out for Cloud.

The horse sniffed the apple but didn't take it.

"I thought horses were supposed to like apples," Kate said. "Oh well, more for me." She bit into an apple, crunching loudly. "My legs are tired." Kate looked around for somewhere to sit.

A short distance away, she spied a big black rock. "Let's rest over there," she said.

Kate peered at the rock. Was she imagining things, or had it just moved?

The rock stretched, growing larger.

Kate froze, stifling a cry. That was no rock. It was a bear!

The bear rose to its feet. Kate hoped it hadn't noticed them in the mist. If they could hide somewhere, maybe they'd be safe. Kate glanced around. The only thing she saw was the apple tree.

The bear started to lumber towards them. Kate dropped the apples she was holding and slowly moved behind the tree. She stood as still as a statue, afraid to run and draw the bear's attention. Maybe, by some miracle, it would pass them by.

The bear advanced until it was so close she could hear it grunting. She could see the droplets of mist on its thick black fur.

Reaching the apple tree, the bear rose on its hind legs. It lifted its giant paw to strike....

At a beehive! Kate almost laughed out loud in relief. The bear was only reaching for the beehive hanging from a branch!

The hive fell to the ground, spilling honey. Angry bees swarmed around the tree. They buzzed through the mist, darkening the orchard. One of them stung Kate on her arm. She covered the sting with her hand and gritted her teeth. They had to get out of there!

The bear was digging its paw into the hive. Kate saw her chance. She rushed to Cloud and scrambled up on to her back. "Go!" she murmured. "Go!"

Without a backwards glance, they raced away.

When she thought they had gone far enough, Kate caught her breath. "Whoa!" she told Cloud. "Slow down now."

She grinned as Cloud slowed to a walk. How well Cloud understood her!

"I wish you could be my horse, always," Kate said.

Ahead, Kate saw a wide, rushing river – the biggest one she'd ever seen in Never Land.

It must be Wough River, she thought, *the big river that runs from Torth Mountain to the sea.* Kate hadn't been there before, but she'd heard the fairies talk about it. She knew she was far from Pixie Hollow. It would take her ages to walk back.

That is, if I can even find my way, Kate thought. She realized she'd been wrong when she'd spoken to Vidia – she had no idea which direction Pixie Hollow was in. All the landmarks she'd passed were hidden in the fog.

For the first time since she'd left Pixie Hollow with Cloud, Kate started to feel worried. She knew she needed to find her way home as quickly as possible.

And yet she hesitated. The truth was, she wasn't ready to say goodbye to Cloud.

Cloud suddenly lifted her head. She looked alert.

"What is it?" Kate asked.

A whinny rang out from across the river. Then another. It was the herd! Kate nudged the horse with her heels.

When they reached the edge of the water, Cloud didn't even pause. The fast-moving water frothed around her hooves as she charged across. Kate couldn't tell if the river was shallow or if Cloud was actually striding across the surface.

Within moments, Cloud was scrambling up the far bank. The herd was just ahead. Kate's thoughts of returning to Pixie Hollow melted away.

chapter 8

As the day wore on, Silvermist tried her best to follow the trails through the damp grass. But doubts constantly tugged at her mind. Sometimes the trail disappeared. Other times it seemed to go in two directions at once. And, as Mia had pointed out, were they even really following Kate? With every turn, Silvermist doubted her choices.

If only there were some way to be sure!

Once, when Silvermist peered through the fog, she thought she saw a dark-haired fairy flying fast.

"Vidia!" she called, hoping the fairy might have seen Kate. "Is that you?"

But if Vidia heard her, she didn't reply.

At last, in a valley, Silvermist lost the trail completely. She stopped and looked around. A short distance away stood a crooked old apple tree. A broken beehive lay on the ground beneath it. A few bees buzzed around the tree.

Silvermist was tired. Her wings ached. She could see that the girls were exhausted, too.

"It's useless!" Mia complained, flopping down to the ground. "Kate's on a horse. We'll never catch up with her." Her forehead furrowed. "It's just like Kate to go running off and leave us behind to worry about her."

"We can't give up," Silvermist said.

"Mia's right," Lainey agreed. "We should go back to Pixie Hollow and wait for Kate there. After all, Never Land is an island. If she goes round it, she'll end up back there eventually. Right?"

"There's a part of the legend I didn't tell you," Silvermist said. "I didn't want you to be afraid. But Kate is in danger. According to the legend, once the mist horse has a rider, it never lets her go. It will spirit her away to the clouds – forever."

The girls stared at her, wide-eyed. "That means we might never see Kate again?" Lainey whispered.

Mia leaped to her feet. "We have to go now!"

At that moment, they saw a large, dark shape coming towards them through the mist. *Not a horse,* Silvermist thought, peering at it. *Something bigger....*

"Bear!" Gabby gasped.

"Run!" cried Mia.

"No! Don't!" Lainey whispered. "That will make it want to chase you."

The girls froze. The bear was coming closer. It was just metres away from them now.

"I'm scared," said Gabby.

"Somebody *do* something!" hissed Mia.

Silvermist fluttered in distress. She was only a tiny fairy! How could she stop a huge bear? Maybe she could throw an apple at it? Or should she fly right at the bear and try to distract it? She flittered back and forth, unsure what to do.

Just then, she heard a string of high-pitched squeaks. Silvermist looked around. She realized the squeaks were coming from Lainey.

The bear heard them, too. It rose on to its hind legs and sniffed the air. It seemed confused.

A moment passed, then Lainey squeaked again. The bear turned and lumbered away.

The girls stayed frozen until the bear was out of sight. Then everyone breathed out a sigh of relief. "I didn't know you could speak Bear!" Mia said to Lainey.

"I can't," Lainey admitted. "I was speaking Mouse. I don't know why – it just came out."

"What did you say?" Gabby asked.

Lainey grinned sheepishly. "I said, 'I've lost my brothers and sisters. There are 20 more like me. Have you seen them?'"

"He probably thought you were the biggest mouse he'd ever seen," Silvermist said with a chuckle.

Everyone laughed. But their laughter quickly faded. "Is Kate going to be okay?" Gabby asked.

Lainey glanced at Silvermist with a worried look.

"I hope so," said Silvermist.

Mia was collecting apples from the tree. Suddenly, she stopped and sucked in her breath. "Look!" she said, holding an apple core up by its stem. "It's been eaten. And not by a bear."

"It could have been Kate!" Lainey said. "That means she did pass through here!"

Silvermist looked to the far end of the valley. "I think Wough River is just ahead. She'll have to stop to rest at some point. Let's hope we can catch her there."

When they reached the river, Silvermist landed on Gabby's shoulder. They stood on the rocky bank, looking at the water rushing past. Silvermist took a deep breath and let the sound soothe her nerves. Water always made her feel calmer.

"She's not here," Mia said, looking as if she might cry. "And how will we ever get across?" The shore on the other side of the river was nearly lost in the fog.

"Hello?" came a voice from the mist.

Silvermist looked around. No one was there.

"Silvermist?"

"Did you call me?" Silvermist asked the girls.

They all shook their heads. *Am I hearing things?* wondered Silvermist.

"It's me." The fog swirled in front of Silvermist. She made out the shape of one wing, then another. Then Myka appeared. She was wearing a cotton top and trousers and a cotton-ball hat. "I'm in camouflage so predators won't see me. You can't be too careful in this fog," she explained.

"Have you seen Kate?" Mia asked quickly.

Myka shook her head. "I haven't seen anyone except Vidia. And even she was on her way back to Pixie Hollow. The fog seems to be worse over here."

So it was Vidia I saw, thought Silvermist.

"The mist is retreating around Pixie Hollow," Myka said. "The Home Tree is all clear. Maybe that means the fog is leaving Never Land."

The girls looked stricken. "Oh, no. Kate!" said Mia.

"What is it?" Myka asked.

Silvermist explained the myth to Myka. "But maybe there's still time," she said. Being near the water was helping her think more clearly. "The fog follows the mist horses. And it's as thick as we've seen it here. Perhaps that's a sign that the horses are nearby. And maybe Kate is with them."

"Do you really think so?" Lainey asked.

Silvermist took a deep breath. Even though she'd made mistakes, she'd got the girls this far.

"I'm almost sure of it," she told the other girls.

Lainey squinted at the water. "Okay," she said slowly. "But how do we get to the other side?"

chapter 9

The river was wide and the current strong. Silvermist knew the girls couldn't swim across. And they couldn't fly like fairies.

She looked around. Her eyes fell on the remains of an old tree that had fallen upstream. It looked almost long enough to stretch from one bank to the other.

"Maybe we could use that log as a bridge," she said.

The girls walked up to the log and strained to lift it. It didn't budge.

"Good thing I have a little extra fairy dust," said Myka. "This will lighten our load." She sprinkled the dust on the log.

"One, two, three, lift!" shouted Silvermist.

The girls raised the log easily. It stood straight up like a telegraph pole.

"Now let it drop!" Silvermist cried.

They did, and the log fell across the river with a huge splash. Silvermist grinned. She'd been right about the length. The far end landed on the opposite shore.

Lainey eyed the log nervously. "It looks slippery."

"That's one thing I can help with," Silvermist said. Using her water magic, she drew water from the wood, drying the top of the log. A stream of droplets trailed behind her like a banner until the tree's surface was dry.

"I'll go in front," Mia said. "Gabby, stay right behind me."

Mia stepped out on to the log. Gabby followed, flapping her arms. "If I start to fall, I can use my wings."

Mia grimaced as the log trembled. "Be careful, Gabby. Remember, some of us don't *have* wings."

"We can think of it like a balance beam," Lainey said. "Like in gymnastics class at school."

Silvermist had no idea what Lainey was talking about. She knew the girls went to school on the mainland. Maybe they learned how to walk on logs there.

The girls put one foot in front of the other, stepping carefully. Slowly, they made their way across.

"Look at me, Silvermist!" Gabby giggled. "I'm a balance-talent fairy!"

Mia hopped off the log, landing on the muddy bank. Laughing, Gabby leaped into her waiting arms. But as she did, her feet pushed the log away from the shore.

"Ahhh!" screamed Lainey, who hadn't quite reached the end. Her arms flailed. She began to lose her balance.

"Jump!" cried Silvermist.

Lainey leaped as the log broke free. Her feet splashed down in the water, but her hands landed in the mud on the bank. Mia and Gabby scrambled to pull her onshore.

"Are you okay?" Mia asked.

"I think so," Lainey said shakily as she climbed to her feet. She looked down at her soaked jeans and dirty shirt. "Just wet – and muddy. Yuck!" She grinned up at Mia. "I don't know how we're going to explain *this* to your parents when they wake up."

Mia grinned back, and Silvermist sighed with relief. That had been a close one.

"Do we go left, right or straight on?" Lainey asked, turning to Silvermist.

Silvermist looked around. The fog was thicker than ever to her right.

She was sure now that her guess about the horses had been correct.

"Follow me!" she said.

*

Kate's heart thudded. Cloud had climbed up a steep, narrow trail. They were close to the herd. That meant they were close to the end of their journey, too.

She could hear the horses, but she couldn't see them. High whinnies and low nickers echoed through the mist. The fog was so thick here, it was like walking through cotton. The ground beneath them felt thin and rocky – Kate could hear stones clattering beneath Cloud's hooves. A chilly wind was blowing.

Then, suddenly, Kate saw the herd. The horses all lifted their heads to watch Kate and Cloud's approach. In the swirling mist, the animals looked ghostly.

Cloud rode Kate into the centre of the herd. The horses circled them, some of them nuzzling Cloud in greeting. An electric feeling coursed through Kate. Was this really happening to her? Even the animal-talent fairy Fawn hadn't been able to talk to the horses. And yet, Kate was being welcomed into their midst.

Kate wished this moment would never end.

But then she heard voices. Not horses, or even fairies, but human voices. At first, she couldn't make out what they were saying. Then, quite clearly, she heard her name: *"K-a-a-ate!"*

It was Mia!

Then she heard Lainey, Gabby and small, thin fairy voices, too. They were all calling out to her.

She couldn't see her friends through all the fog, so she steered Cloud towards the sound of their voices. Suddenly, Cloud stopped so fast that Kate fell forward against her mane. Cloud's front hoof dislodged a stone. Kate listened as it bounced down ... and down ... and down.

At that moment, the wind shifted, briefly clearing the mist. Kate gasped. She and Cloud stood at the edge of a narrow ledge. Before them lay a deep, rocky canyon. On the other side of the canyon were Kate's friends, separated from her by the huge chasm.

Mia, Lainey and Gabby were waving and screaming. Now she could hear their cries more clearly.

"Get away from there, Kate! The horse is ... "

Kate couldn't hear the rest. She tried to get Cloud to back up, but the herd was crowded in behind them. There was nowhere to go.

Cloud took a step forward. They were going to fall!

"No!" shouted Mia.

"Stop!" cried Lainey.

"Kate!" screamed Gabby.

But it was too late. Cloud stepped off the edge.

chapter 10

Kate squeezed her eyes shut. She was expecting to drop like a stone. Instead, she felt a gentle wind against her face.

Kate opened her eyes. Cloud was galloping in the air high above the canyon. They were flying!

Cloud rode the wind. Legs pumping, she climbed up above the fog right into the clear blue sky.

Kate couldn't say a word. She was breathless with excitement. They were really and truly flying!

The other mist horses galloped around them. With a sound like rolling thunder, the herd stampeded across the sky.

At last, Kate found her voice. She cried out, a loud, joyful whoop. She felt like the queen of the sky!

Just when it seemed as if they might leave the ground for good, Cloud began to turn. The herd followed. They raced back and landed lightly on the narrow strip of land, across the chasm from where they'd come. Cloud had brought Kate to her friends.

Kate slid off the mist horse and grinned. "Did you guys see that?"

"Kate!" Mia rushed over and wrapped her in a hug. Lainey and Gabby joined her. "You're all right!"

"Of course I'm all right," said Kate, surprised. "Why wouldn't I be? And what are you all doing here anyway?"

"We thought the horse had kidnapped you!" Gabby said.

"You mean Cloud?" Kate patted the horse's neck. "Of course not. She's my new best friend."

Silvermist and the other girls explained everything – the mist horse legend, the scary thought that Kate might be spirited away and the long journey they'd taken to find her.

"I was afraid we'd never find you, after my many wrong turns," Silvermist said. "I even went to the beach, thinking you might be there."

"I *did* go to the beach," Kate said. "Before I went to Vine Grove."

"Silvermist, you were right all along," Lainey said.

Myka smiled at her water-talent

friend. "It seems you're a better tracker than you realize."

Silvermist's glow turned pink as she blushed at the compliment. "So I guess the legend was wrong," she said. "The mist horses aren't dangerous. I wonder how that idea ever came to be."

"I'll bet I know," said Kate. "Maybe once upon a time someone *did* ride away with the mist horses forever. After riding with Cloud, I can understand why they would want to." Kate laughed as Cloud nuzzled her cheek. "But I can't believe you were worried. My horse would never do anything bad."

Mia looked puzzled. "Did you just say *my* horse?"

Kate gave a sheepish smile. "I guess I did. And in a way, she is mine – like I'm hers. But just now, when we were riding, flying up in the air, I realized Cloud doesn't need a rider. She needs to be free. She needs to run wild with her herd."

Kate hugged the mist horse round the neck, holding on tightly for a long moment. Then she stepped back. "Go on now," she said. "Go be with your friends. I'll never forget you."

Cloud looked Kate in the eye and whinnied. Then she took off, climbing into the sky once again. The other horses galloped towards her. They met in a flurry of hooves and mist. Together, they raced away.

"Look!" Silvermist exclaimed. "The fog is lifting!"

The mist rose like a curtain. They could see the landscape clearly now: the cliffs, the canyons and the sea in the distance.

Kate, her friends and the fairies watched the horses until all they could see were the last thin wisps of their tails trailing across the sky.

"Those clouds will be bringing rain," Silvermist added. "We should get back to the Home Tree." She winked at Gabby. "Before our wings get wet and we can't fly."

Gabby laughed. "You know I can't fly without fairy dust! Anyway, I'd rather walk with Kate." She reached for Kate's hand.

Kate squeezed Gabby's hand in her own. She was glad to be back with her friends. And in a way, she was glad to have two feet on solid ground again.

"What about you, Kate?" Silvermist asked. "Are you ready?"

Kate nodded. "I've had enough adventure for one day." She smiled at Silvermist. "Lead the way."

Don't miss the next magical
book in the Never Girls series,
Wedding Wings!

Gabby Vasquez hurried up the stairs
to her room. She had news – the kind of
fizzy, exciting news that wouldn't stay
bottled up inside. She just had to tell
someone about it!

In her bedroom, Gabby raced to the
wardrobe. She threw the door open wide,
shouting, "Guess what, everyone?"

She stepped inside, closing the door
behind her. The wardrobe was very dark,
but it was a friendly sort of darkness.
She could smell orange blossoms and
hear water trickling over rocks.

Gabby shuffled forward. She saw a
window of light, then she emerged into
the sunshine of Pixie Hollow.

Hop-two-three. Gabby skipped from rock to rock, crossing Havendish Stream. She wriggled between two wild rose bushes on the far bank. Her costume fairy wings caught on a thorn. Gabby quickly checked to make sure the fabric hadn't ripped. Then she plunged ahead, stumbling a little in her hurry.

As she came over a small rise, she could see the Home Tree, the great maple where the Never fairies worked and lived. The fairies' golden glows shone among the leaves, making it seem as if the branches were filled with stars.

"Tink! Prilla! Everybody! Guess what?" Gabby shouted.

On a high branch, the art-talent fairy Bess looked up from her painting. Prilla, the clapping-talent fairy, awoke from her doze in a cosy magnolia blossom.

The pots-and-pans fairy Tinker Bell stuck her head out of her tea-kettle workshop. The garden fairy Rosetta set down her miniature gourd watering can. And Dulcie, a baking-talent fairy, dusted the flour from her hands. They all flew to the courtyard.

"What's going on?" Prilla asked as Gabby ran up to them, breathless.

Gabby bounced on her toes with excitement. "There's going to be a wedding," she announced. "And I'm the star!"

"A wedding?" cried Dulcie, wringing her apron. "Why didn't anyone tell me? I haven't baked a thing!"

"Not here, silly," Gabby said. "At home. Our babysitter Julia is getting married, and I'm going to be the flower girl!"

"Is that anything like being a flower-talent fairy?" Rosetta asked.

"Kind of," said Gabby. "I'm in charge of all the flower magic. And I get to wear this special dress." She did a twirl so the fairies could admire her brand-new pretty pink flower-girl dress.

"It's lovely!" exclaimed Rosetta, who adored dresses of all kinds.

"I have this basket, too." Gabby held up a little basket with a bow tied round the handle. "And I throw flower petals. Like this." Gabby pretended to pull a handful of petals from the basket and throw them.

"Hmm." Rosetta frowned.

Gabby stopped. "What's the matter?"

"Why not practise with some *real* flowers?" Rosetta suggested. She plucked a bundle of daisies that were growing nearby and shook the petals into Gabby's basket.

Gabby threw a few of the petals. They plopped to the ground.

"Well," said Tink, "that's not very interesting."

"Wouldn't it be nicer if the petals moved around a little?" suggested Bess. She dived into the basket and came up with an armful of petals. When she threw them into the air, they swirled like snowflakes.

Gabby gasped. "How did you do that?"

"It's easy. You just need a bit of fairy magic." Bess shook her wings over the basket. A sprinkle of fairy dust rained down on the petals. "Try it again."

This time the petals almost leaped from Gabby's hand. They fluttered in the air before drifting to the ground.

The fairies nodded happily.

"Oh, yes!"

"Much nicer!"

"Just lovely."

Gabby smiled and threw another handful just to watch the petals swirl. "Can I have some fairy dust to take with me to the wedding tomorrow? Please?"

"I don't see why not," Tink said. She darted away. In a moment she was back with a little thimble bucket. It had a tight-fitting silver lid. "I made the lid myself," Tink said proudly. "You won't lose a speck of dust."

Gabby peeked inside and saw the shimmery fairy dust. "Thank you," she said, tucking the thimble into the pocket of her dress.

"I've heard of weddings, but I've never seen one," said Prilla. She travelled to the world of Clumsies – or humans – more than most fairies. "What are they like?"

"A wedding is when two people get married," Gabby told her. "They say 'I love you.' Then they give each other rings and everybody claps. And then …" Here, Gabby's knowledge of weddings became somewhat murky, but she continued, "Then they float away on a cloud and live happily ever after!"

"Very dramatic," Bess said, nodding her head approvingly.

"Will there be food at the wedding?" Dulcie asked.

"Yes! Really fancy food, like onion rings. And a cake this big!" Gabby stretched her hands up over her head. To the fairies, the cake seemed enormous.

"My!" Dulcie exclaimed.

"Will there be music and dancing?" Tinker Bell asked. "At fairy parties there's always dancing."

Gabby had no idea if there was dancing at a wedding. But her imagination had taken over now. "Everybody dances! And there are butterflies everywhere! And a chocolate waterfall!" Gabby spun on her toes, inspired by her own vision of how wonderful the wedding would be.

Prilla's freckled face took on a dreamy look. "It sounds marvellous. I wish I could see it."

"You could come with me!" Gabby suggested.

Don't miss the sixth magical
book in the Never Girls series,
The Woods Beyond!

Ever since four friends – Lainey
Winters, Kate McCrady, Mia Vasquez
and Mia's little sister, Gabby – discovered
a secret passage to Never Land, each day
held the possibility of a new adventure.
They woke up in the morning feeling
like the luckiest girls in the world.
Most mornings, that is.

"Lainey!"

Lainey Winters opened her eyes.
Her mother was calling her. She reached
out, feeling around for her glasses.
Her hand touched the wooden bedside
table where she always left them.

But her glasses weren't there.

"Lainey!" her mother yelled again.

"Come down here!"

Lainey got out of bed. Without her glasses, everything looked blurry. Where could she have left them?

As she fumbled across the room, she stubbed her toe, hard. "Ow!" Lainey cried. Blinking back tears, she hopped on one foot to her chest of drawers and felt around on top. Her glasses weren't there, either.

The bedroom door opened. "Didn't you hear me?" her mother asked. "I've been calling you for the last five minutes." She frowned. "Where are your glasses?"

"I don't know." Lainey looked around helplessly. "Somewhere …"

"Not another lost pair," her mother said with a sigh. "You'll have to wear the spare ones."

It was Lainey's turn to frown. She *hated* her spare glasses. Her regular big, square glasses were bad enough. But the spare ones were broken and had been fixed with tape. In Lainey's opinion, they just looked dumb.

"When you're ready, come downstairs. There's something I want you to see." Her mother left.

Lainey found the old glasses in her desk drawer. *Why couldn't* these *be lost?* she wondered. Then she got dressed and went downstairs. Her mother was standing in the kitchen with her arms folded across her chest.

"Look outside," she said to Lainey.

Lainey looked out of the window. "Oh, no!" she exclaimed.

In front of their house, the rubbish and recycling cans lay on their sides. The bin bags inside had been ripped open and rubbish was scattered around their garden. More rubbish was strewn along the pavement. "What happened?" Lainey asked.

"Some animals must have got into the bins," her mother replied. "Did you leave those dishes out last night, Lainey?"

Every morning in summer, Lainey filled two big bowls with dog food and water and left them on the pavement in front of their house for any dogs that passed. Lainey didn't have a dog, but she tried to get to know all the pets in her neighbourhood. She liked to help out her furry friends whenever she could.

Lainey's parents didn't want a pet of their own, so they didn't mind the bowls. But the rule was that she had to bring them in at night.

And she *had* brought them in, hadn't she?